TO: daddy

Love

ELVIS PRESLEY'S

Love Me Tender

To our loving son, Michael,
and his beautiful daughter, Jordan.
—T.B.

"Love Me Tender" by Elvis Presley and Vera Matson
Copyright © 1956 by Elvis Presley Music, Inc.
Copyright Renewed and Assigned to Elvis Presley Music
International Copyright Secured. Reprinted by Permission.
Illustrations copyright © 2003 by Tom Browning
Manufactured in China. All Rights Reserved.
www.harperchildrens.com

Library of Congress Cataloging-in-Publication Data
Presley, Elvis, 1935–1977.
Elvis Presley's Love me tender / lyrics by Elvis Presley
and Vera Matson ; illustrated by Tom Browning.
p.   cm. Summary: A father and daughter share their
special bond through Elvis Presley's timeless lyrics.
ISBN 0-06-027797-1
1. Children's songs—United States—Texts. [1. Love—Songs and music.
2. Songs.] I. Title: Love me tender. II. Matson, Vera.
III. Browning, Tom, 1949– ill. IV. Title.
PZ8.3.P912 El 2003   2002018936
782.42164'0268—dc21

Typography by Stephanie Bart-Horvath
1 2 3 4 5 6 7 8 9 10
❖
First Edition

ELVIS PRESLEY'S

Love Me Tender

Lyrics by Elvis Presley and Vera Matson

Illustrated by Tom Browning

HarperCollins*Publishers*

Love me tender,
love me sweet;
Never let me go.

You have made
my life complete,
And I love you so.

Love me tender,
love me true,
All my dreams
fulfill.

For, my darlin',
I love you,
And I always will.

Love me tender,
love me long;
Take me to your heart.

For it's there
that I belong,
And we'll never part.

Love me tender,
love me true,
All my dreams
fulfill.

For, my darlin',
I love you,
And I always will.

Love me tender,
love me dear;
Tell me you are mine.

I'll be yours
through all the years,
Till the end of time.

Love me tender,
love me true,
All my dreams
fulfill.

For, my darlin',
I love you,

And I always will.